LITTLE CRITTER'S®
THESE ARE MY PETS

BY
MERCER MAYER

To Genevieve

A Golden Book • New York
Western Publishing Company, Inc., Racine, Wisconsin 53404

This is my frog.
He is green.

He likes to sit
in water.
I like to sit
in water.

He likes to hop.
I like to hop.

My frog is my friend.

This is my turtle.
He is green, too.

He likes to hide
in the grass.
I like to hide
in the grass.
My turtle is my friend.

This is my fish.
My fish is yellow.

She likes to swim.
I like to swim.

I like to look
at my fish.
My fish likes
to look at me.

My fish is my friend.

This is my dog.
My dog is brown and white.

My dog likes to run.
I like to run.

My dog likes to dig.
I like to dig.

My dog is my friend.

This is my kitten.
She is black and white.

She likes my dog.
She likes his tail
best of all.

My kitten likes
my frog, too.

My kitten likes
to sit in the sun.
I like to sit
in the sun.
My kitten is my friend.

This is my bug.
My bug is black.

My bug likes to fly.
I like to see
my bug fly.

My bug likes
to sit on my hand.

I keep my bug in a jar.
I like my bug.
My bug is my friend.

This is my snake.
My snake is green and yellow.

I keep my snake
in a cage.

My snake can move fast.
I can move fast.
My snake is my friend.

When I take a bath,
my friends want
to take a bath, too.
But Mom says, "No."

When I get in bed,
my friends get in bed, too.
But Mom says, "No.
No pets in bed.

Just say good night
and go to sleep."

So my frog says good night.
My dog says good night.
My kitten says good night.

My other friends don't
say a thing.

I say good night
to my friends.
And we all go to sleep.